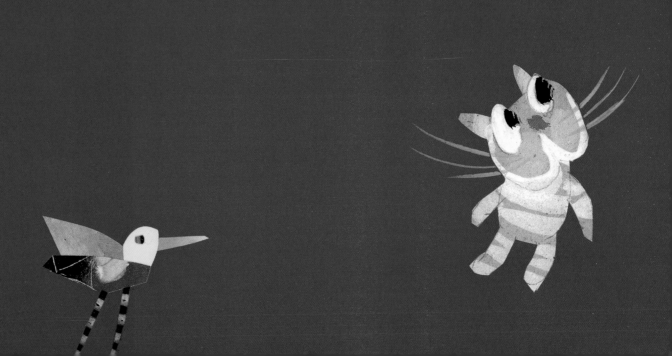

Bling Blang

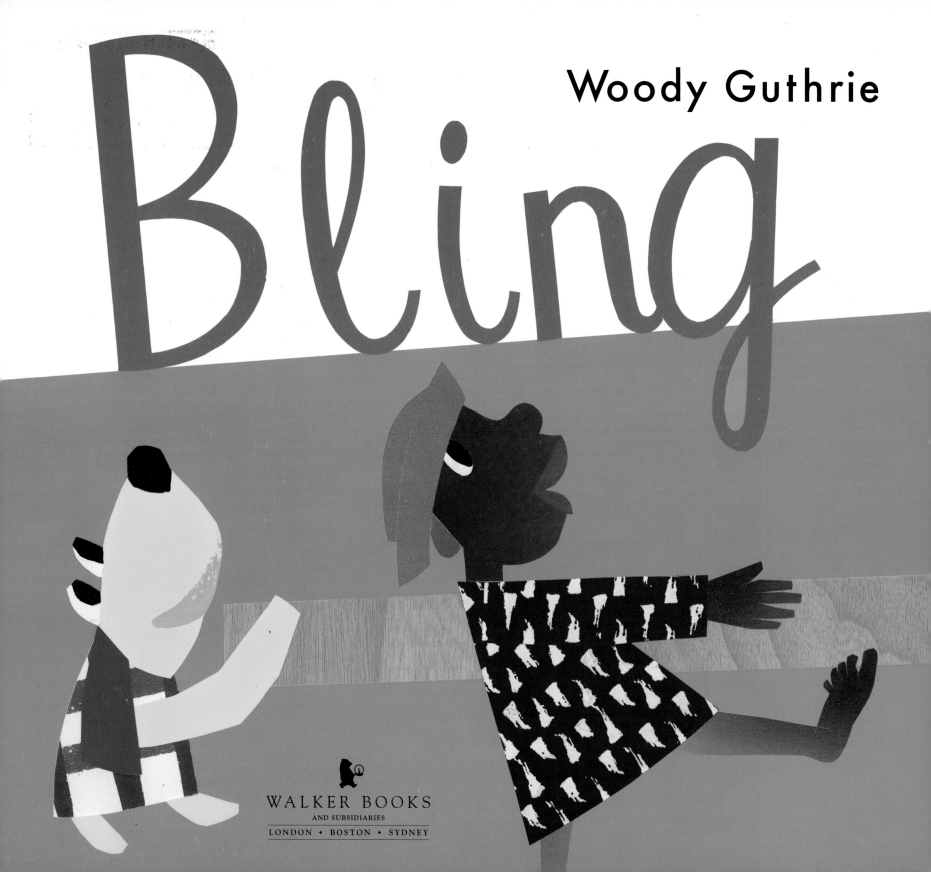

Bling

Woody Guthrie

WALKER BOOKS
AND SUBSIDIARIES
LONDON • BOSTON • SYDNEY

Blang

pictures by **Vladimir Radunsky**

You get a hammer and I'll get a nail;
You catch a bird and I'll catch a snail;

You bring a board and I'll bring a saw,
And we'll build a house for the baby-o.

Zing-o Zang-o,

Cutting with my saw.

I'll grab some mud and you grab some clay
So when it rains it won't wash away.

We'll build a house that'll be so strong,
The winds will sing my baby a song.

Chorus:

Bling blang,
Hammer with my hammer,

Zing-o zang-o,
Cutting with my saw.

Run bring rocks and I'll bring bricks.
A nice pretty house we'll build and fix.

We'll jump inside when the cold wind blows
And kiss our pretty little baby-o.

Chorus:

**Bling blang,
Hammer with my hammer,**

**Zing-o zang-o,
Cutting with my saw.**

You bring a ladder and I'll get a box.
Build our house out of bricks and blocks.

When the snowbird flies and the honeybee comes,
We'll feed our baby on honey in the comb.

Bling blang,

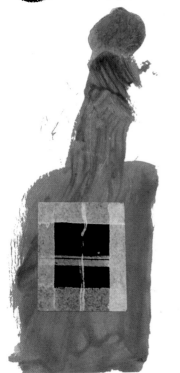

A Lexandra's Tower

Sasha's House

another Sasha's House

hammer with my hammer

Emma's House

HOLLY's houses

ANna's house

Husband and WIFe

Zing-o Zang-o,

COLIN'S TOWER

COLIN'S HOUSE

Cutting with my saw

Nathaniel's house

PATiupa house

Alexandra's Tower

For Shel Silverstein, Master Builder — N. G.

Special thanks to Ann Stott for her invaluable
help and patience during this project — V. R.

Thank you, Colin Meret, thank you, Emma Bridges
thank you, Holly Bridges, thank you, Nathaniel Santoro
thank you, Patiupa Brodsky, thank you, Anna Radunsky
thank you, Sasha Radunsky, thank you, Quintan Stott
for the beautiful drawings and paintings you've done
for the book — V. R.

The publisher wishes to acknowledge the help and
support of Nora Guthrie and Judy Bell; and
Bing Broderick of Rounder Records in the
publication of this book.

First published 2000 by Walker Books Ltd
87 Vauxhall Walk, London SE11 5HJ

10 9 8 7 6 5 4 3 2 1

Illustrations © 2000 Vladimir Radunsky

This book has been typeset in Futura.